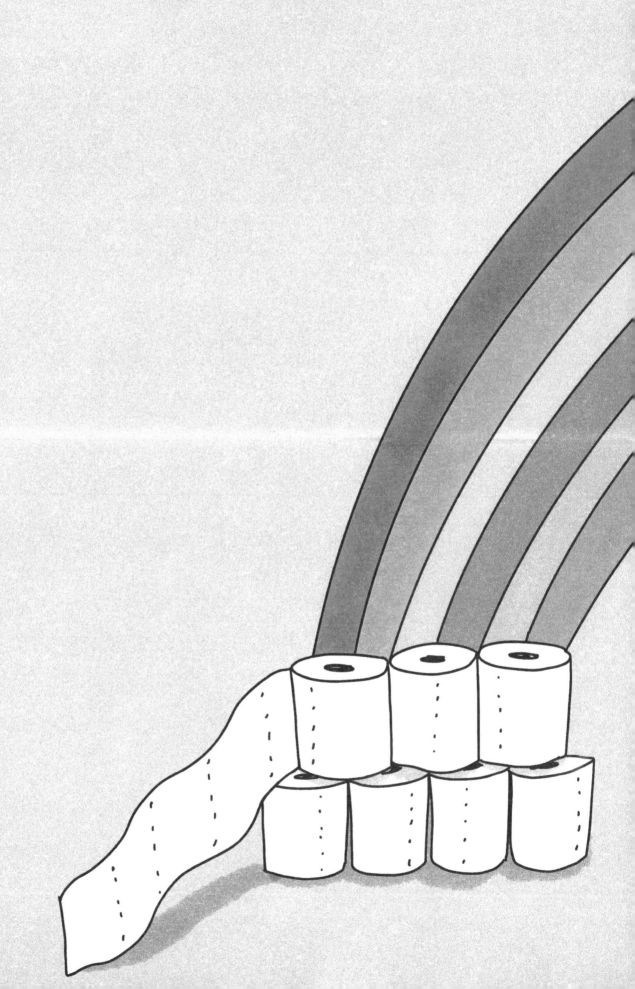

To all the little human beings of the world. May you find peace
in troubled times. May you breathe and stay positive. And to all
the essential helpers and miracle workers who are healing the sick,
staying calm in line ups, and having patio concerts. Thank you for
bringing our world peace. – JK

For Wendell, our sweet quarantine baby. – CM

when the world PANICS

written by Jillian Knuttila

illustrated by Catherine Moyer

One day, the world panicked. Lilly did not know what to do.

Everywhere she looked, adults around her were panicking. They used to be happy. They used to be calm. But everything was different now.

Her teachers weren't smiling anymore.

Her parents had less patience than normal.

Even people in the grocery store were mad.

Then, Lilly heard some startling news:
"Schools are closed indefinitely."

She didn't know what that word meant, so she
decided to look it up in the dictionary. Indefinitely
means: for an unknown amount of time.

Lilly was shocked at this announcement. She loved school!
What would she do without school? Her brother Lyndon, on
the other hand, was thrilled. Now, he had more time to play.

Apparently the world was panicking because you couldn't play with other people right now. Everyone had to stay home and keep their germs to themselves.

Lilly and Lyndon couldn't even play with their cousins who lived across the street. Sometimes they would do sidewalk chalk on their driveways and yell to one another.

Some days it felt like there was nothing to do. Lilly's mom did not like them to say, "I'm bored." So, Lilly tried to stay busy. She started by looking at her tablet.

But after scrolling through her favourite sites, she realized that they were all about the big panic. That made her nervous. So, she unplugged her black box and decided to play with real boxes instead.

"Lyndon!" Lilly called, "Let's make forts!" Lyndon came running and soon their cardboard creations filled the living room. Lyndon combined the tallest boxes with all of his lacrosse sticks to make a tree fort. He imagined that he was Robin Hood.

Lilly created a rainbow castle. It even had a watery moat and fluffy clouds for the rainbow gate.

But, as Lilly and Lyndon played, she remembered the reason why she had so many supplies to make the clouds with. And that reminded her of how everyone was panicking.

Lilly had a lot of questions:

She went to ask her dad, but he was in the middle of watching the news. It was full of more panic, and it was not helpful.

So, Lilly went to ask her mom.

But, her mom was busy working from home. She only had a moment to talk to Lilly and quickly said, "You'll be fine, Lillian."

She wished that she could see her grandma.
Grandma Willow was so wise. She always
knew exactly what to say. But, Lilly wasn't
allowed to see Grandma Willow right now.

She was just about to start moping
around when her mom gave her a
brilliant idea...

"Lilly, why don't you call Grandma? I am sure that she would love to see you."

So, Lilly picked up her tablet and put it to a better use. She called her grandma. And of course, Grandma Willow knew just what to say,

"Lilly, there is a lot of panic in the world right now and the important thing is to not let the adults stress you out. There's something going on that is bigger than you and you are not in control. We are doing the best we can to keep you safe. You are safe. You are loved. You are healthy."

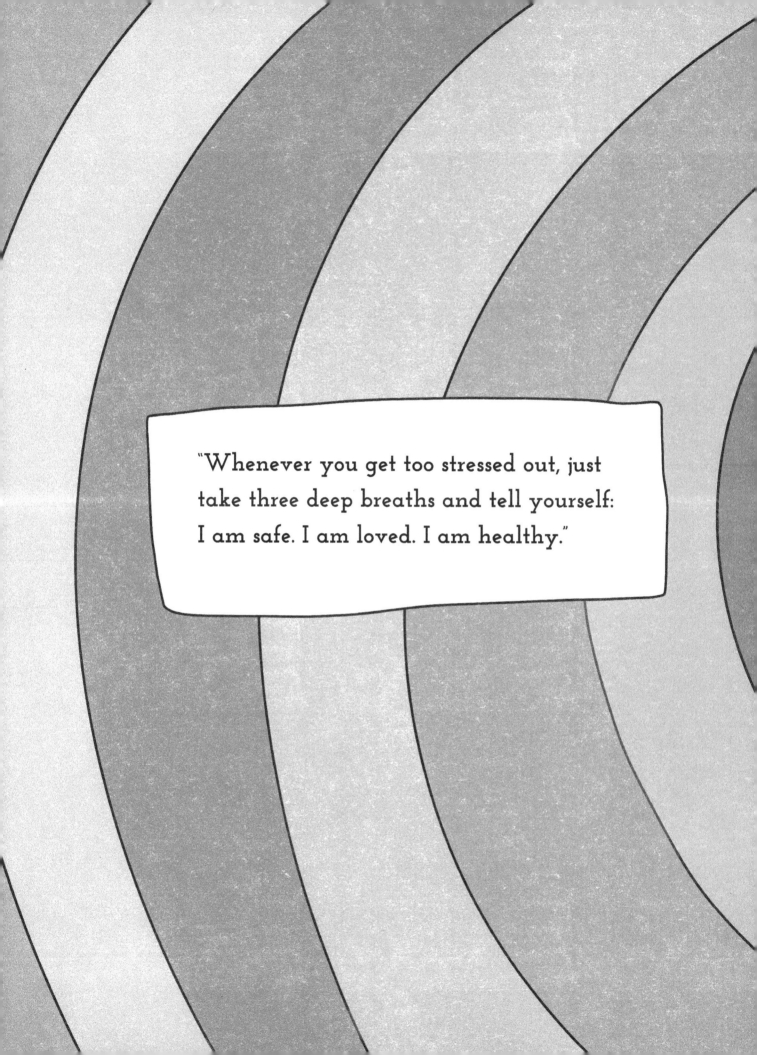

"Whenever you get too stressed out, just take three deep breaths and tell yourself: I am safe. I am loved. I am healthy."

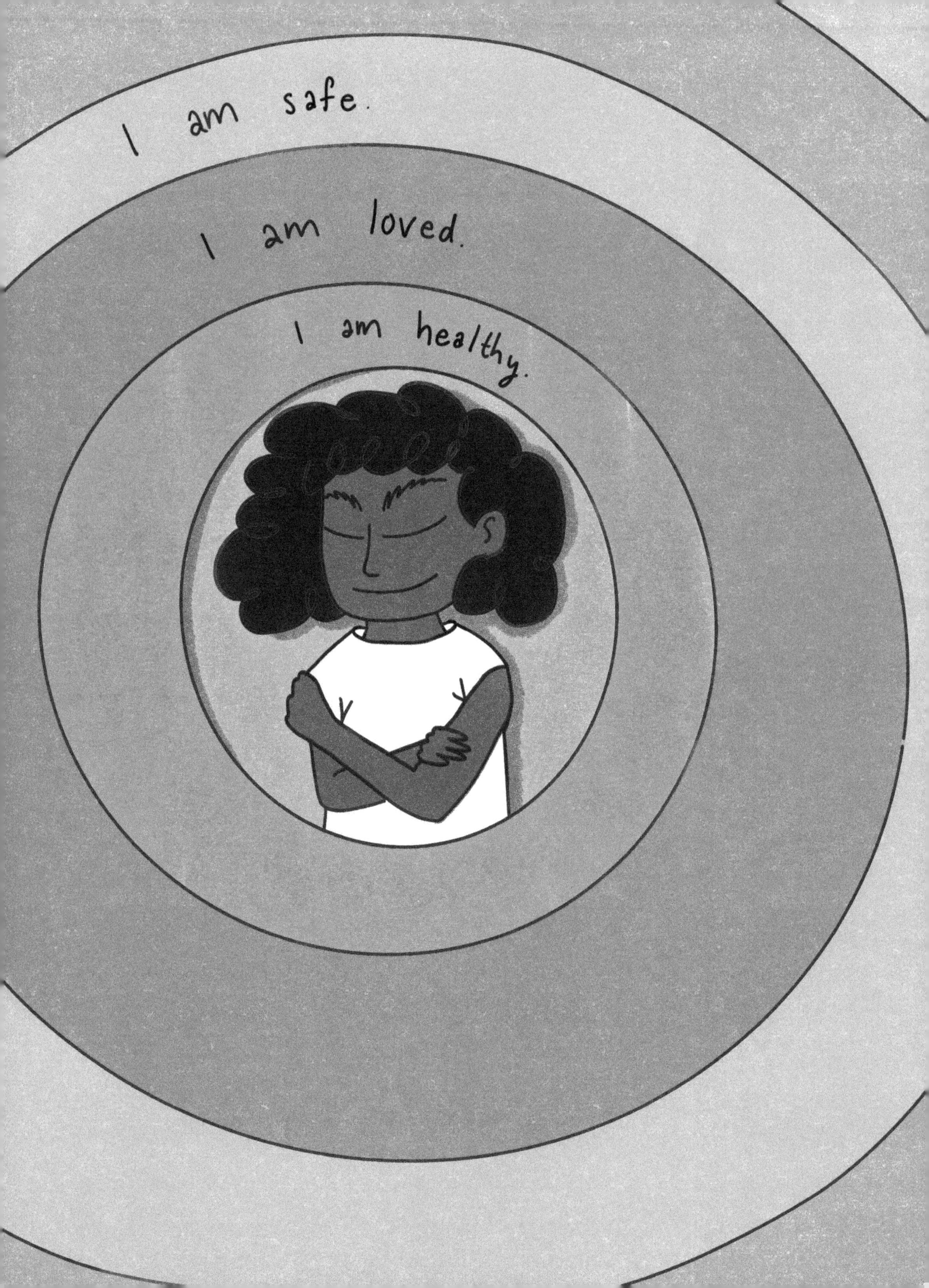
I am safe.
I am loved.
I am healthy.

After thanking Grandma Willow for the fabulous advice, Lilly started getting ready for bed. But, as she had a bath...

And as she brushed her teeth...

...she started thinking about all of the germs again. She felt like she would never be able to get her hands clean enough. Lilly was still feeling the panic.

Sometimes it felt so heavy. It felt like her stomach hurt. It felt like she couldn't breathe. It felt like this big weight that she could not carry.

So, she did what every kid should do when they're feeling this way...

She told a trusted adult.

"Dad, I'm not feeling too good. I'm worried," said Lilly. Dad tucked her in up to her chin and read her a bedtime story. At the end of the story, he said,

"Remember what Grandma told you? Try breathing to calm your mind. Take a deep breath in through your nose and out through your mouth. And take another deep breath in through your nose and out through your mouth. Now, take a third deep breath in through your nose and out through your mouth."

"You are safe.
You are loved.
You are healthy."
With that, Dad kissed her
goodnight on the forehead
and Lilly fell into a
deep, peaceful sleep.

When Lilly woke up the next morning, the world was still
panicking. But, she knew just what to do. Lilly remembered
Grandma Willow's words. She took three deep breaths and
said, "I am safe. I am loved. I am healthy."

Then she found Lyndon and started having another amazing adventure.

When The World Panics . . .
Strategies to Calm Down the Worry

COMFORT – Find a comfortable place, and sit or lay down comfortably. Cross your arms in front of you and give yourself a big hug.

BREATHE – Take three deep breaths: Take a deep breath in through your nose and out through your mouth. And take another deep breath in through your nose and out through your mouth. Now, take a third deep breath in through your nose and out through your mouth.

AFFIRM – Say these words to yourself: I am safe. I am loved. I am healthy. You can use your voice, quietly whisper, or tell yourself in your mind.

RELEASE – Let all of your worries fall off of you. Feel yourself become lighter.

REMEMBER – Anytime you feel the worry starting to come back, remember to comfort yourself, keep breathing, and tell yourself your affirmations.

Jillian Knuttila (BEd, MEd, RDYT200) is a life-long learner and elementary school teacher. She teaches music, library, and yoga. She loves reading, exploring nature, and spending time with her family and friends. She lives in Pitt Meadows, BC.

Catherine Moyer is an illustrator, designer, and musician. She resides in Abbotsford, BC with her husband, Daniel, and son, Wendell. If she's not too busy creating or drinking enough coffee to stay alive, you can reach her at catherineruthdesign@gmail.com.

Jillian and Catherine met in Maple Ridge, BC where they attended elementary school together. They have been friends ever since. This is their first book. For Educator Guides and more, visit: AdventuresofLillyandLyndon.ca.

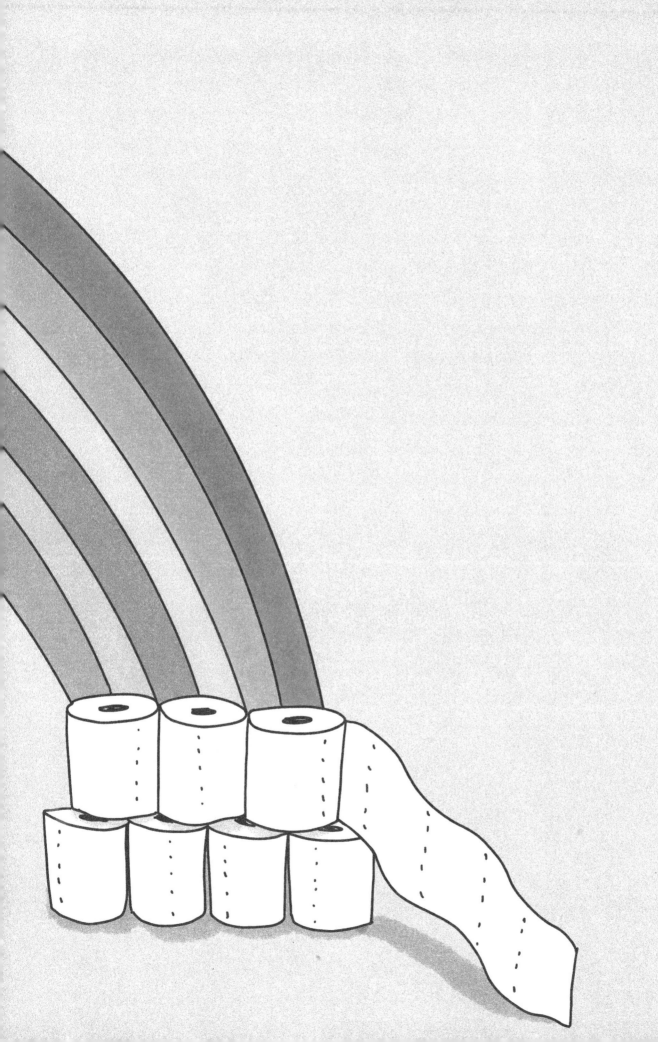

CPSIA information can be obtained
at www.ICGtesting.com
Printed in the USA
LVHW071146120621
690065LV00006B/222